™

IN THE GOOD, THE BAD, AND THE EGGLY

BIG IDEA
BOOKS

www.bigidea.com

Zonder**kidz**™

The children's group of Zondervan

www.zonderkidz.com

Larryboy in the Good, the Bad, and the Eggly
Copyright © 2003 by Big Idea Productions, Inc.

Requests for information should be addressed to:
Zonderkidz, Grand Rapids, Michigan 49530

ISBN: 0-310-70650-5

Written by: Kent Redeker
Editors: Cindy Kenney, Gwen Ellis
Cover and Interior Illustrations: Michael Moore
Cover Design and Art Direction: Big Idea Design
Interior Design: Big Idea Design and Holli Leegwater

CIP applied for
Printed in United States

03 04 05/RRD/5 4 3 2 1

BIG IDEA
BOOKS

IN THE GOOD, THE BAD, AND THE EGGLY

WRITTEN BY
KENT REDEKER

ILLUSTRATED BY
MICHAEL MOORE

BASED ON THE HIT VIDEO SERIES: LARRYBOY
CREATED BY PHIL VISCHER
SERIES ADAPTED BY TOM BANCROFT

Zonderkidz

TABLE OF CONTENTS

CHAPTER 1

FLYING THE SIZZLY SKIES

It was a peaceful night in the skies over Bumblyburg. The air was still with only the gentle flapping of passing pelicans to disturb the lazy clouds floating across the moon.

Not only were the skies peaceful, but they were safe, thanks to Bumblyburg's very own cucumber superhero...Larryboy!

Larryboy was spending the night doing routine patrols over Bumblyburg in his famous Larryplane. And since there was no crime or any other evil-doings afoot in the city tonight, all Larryboy had to do was sit back and relax. He was lucky enough to get a bird's eye view of the city that most of the citizens never got to see.

Some veggies would think that this was a wonderful chance to take in some of the natural beauty that God created.

But not Larryboy. Larryboy was bored.

"Archie!" he whined over the onboard communicator. "How much longer do I have to stay on patrol? There's not a single crime on the Larryscope! Nobody littering, nobody jaywalking, nobody wearing shoes that don't match their pants! Nothing! Why don't we just let police Chief Croswell handle things tonight?"

"But Larryboy," replied Archie, "as Bumblyburg's very own superhero, it's your duty to share the duties of protecting the city."

Archie was Larryboy's confidant, gadget-fixer, and closest friend. Plus, he was the butler of Larryboy's alter ego…Larry the Cucumber.

As such, he was also the only one who had to put up with Larryboy griping about patrol duty.

"But I don't want to share duties tonight! It's *boring*!" said Larryboy. "And boring rhymes with snoring, and snoring is what I do when I'm home in bed, which is where I'd rather be right now."

Archie frowned. He had tried to get Larryboy to take a nap this afternoon, but he wouldn't listen. Master Larry just *had* to stay up playing hopscotch. Archie knew that sharing didn't always seem like the most fun way to do things. But he also knew that in the end, God wants us to share!

"Hey, Archie! The lights are still on at *The Daily Bumble*," Larry said as he zoomed past the building where he worked undercover as the newspaper office janitor.

"Oh, it's just Bob putting the paper to bed," he said as he spied Vicki, the paper's renowned photojournalist. Larryboy smiled dreamily thinking that Vicki was truly the cutest "cuke" in town.

"You know, I think Vicki just might go to the Founder's

Day Party with you this year, if you'd get up the nerve to ask her," suggested Archie.

"Oh yeah, that'll happen, Arch. When pigs fly!" laughed Larryboy.

No sooner had Larryboy finished his sentence, when the Larryplane was attacked! Out of nowhere, three small supersonic objects zoomed past the Larryplane.

SPLAT! SPLAT! SPLAT! Three strips of bacon hit the windshield.

"Oh no! Bacon!" said Larryboy. "Archie, I've been *baconed*!!"

CHAPTER 2

PIGS ON THE WING

"Can you see who is attacking you?" asked Archie.

"Just a second," Larryboy answered as he turned on his windshield wipers to wipe off the greasy bacon while looking through the windshield to see his attackers. What he saw sent shivers through his cucumber body.

Archie had heard Larryboy say many strange things during their time together as crime fighters, but nothing prepared him for what he was about to hear.

"Archie!" said Larryboy. "Pigs *do* fly! I'm being attacked by flying pigs!"

Archie squinted at the images of the flying pigs that were being sent to him through the Larryplane's onboard cameras. While normally, pigs *can't* fly, these three little pigs were strapped into high-tech jet wings that had bacon cannons attached to each side.

"OINK! OINK!" came the sounds from the flying pigs.

"Why would flying pigs

shoot bacon?" asked Archie. "That doesn't make any sense!"

"Archie," said Larryboy, "could we think about that later? Right now I'd like to think about how to make them *stop* shooting bacon!"

The supersonic pigs were closing in...and fast. Larryboy made another quick turn, but this time the pigs stayed right behind him. "OK," said Archie. "The Larrycomputer has just given me some very interesting information. It seems that Willie, Wee-Wee, and Woozy, the three award winning pigs from the town of Maiseville,

were reported missing yesterday. Those pigs must be the pigs that are attacking you!"

Larryboy was about to tell Archie how useless he thought that information was, when another barrage of bacon hit one of the Larryplane's wings, causing the plane to spin out of control.

"AAAAAAH!" cried Larryboy as the plane plummeted towards the ground. "Archie! Something's wrong! I can't see!"

CHAPTER 3
AN EYE-OPENING EXPERIENCE

"Larryboy," said Archie, "open your eyes!"

Larryboy opened one eye, but he didn't like what he saw. The ground was getting closer and closer at an alarming rate. So Larryboy decided to close both eyes again.

Fortunately, Archie had installed a safety feature for just such an event. He had to because Larryboy had a tendency to close his eyes while flying the Larryplane. So, Archie pushed a button on the Larrycomputer and remotely activated the "Larryplane Automatic Anti-Closed-Eyes-Crash System", and the plane pulled up just in time to avoid a crash.

"Is it safe to look yet?" asked Larryboy.

"Yes, Larryboy, it's safe."

Larryboy opened his eyes. "Oh, that's better."

"Can you see where the pigs went?" Archie inquired.

"Yeah. They're not chasing me anymore! They're heading for downtown Bumblyburg."

"Downtown Bumblyburg!" exclaimed Archie. "Larryboy! You've got to stop them before they unleash their bacony assault upon the city!"

As Larryboy turned the Larryplane and raced off after the flying pigs, three dark figures on the ground below looked up to the sky and laughed at the exploits of our hero.

Well, two figures laughed at him. The other figure just sorta stood there.

Who would be so wicked as to chortle with glee in Larryboy's time of desperate need? It was none other than three of Larryboy's most archest-enemies of all: Greta Von Gruesome the Zucchini, Awful Alvin the Onion, and his sidekick, Lampy...the lamp.

"Ha ha!" cackled Awful Alvin. "My villainous plan of villainy is working to perfection!"

"*Your* plan?" said Greta. "You mean *my* plan to distract Larryboy so that no one will be able to stop us as we break into the Bumblyburg Science Labs!"

Lampy just stood there smiling. Lampy always smiled. That's one of the things Awful Alvin liked about him.

Awful Alvin was Bumblyburg's foremost evil genius. For some twisted reason, he just plain enjoyed being bad. He had a secret underground lair, and a burning desire to defeat Larryboy and rule Bumblyburg. Lampy was his faithful henchman. (Little is known about Lampy's background or family history.)

"I think that now is the time when we should perform the villainous dance of villainy to celebrate the villainous deeds we are about to perform!" said Awful Alvin. He grabbed Lampy. "Dance with me, Lampy!"

Greta rolled her eyes. She had agreed to be partners with Awful Alvin, but she wasn't sure it was worth it if

she had to put up with all his dancing and all around oddities. After all, she owned a castle in the mountains outside Bumblyburg. She owned everything she could ever want…including silver-lined power gloves that fired bolts of energy out of the brightly polished fingertips.

But, the fact was, Greta was really greedy, and even with all her riches, she still wanted more! And she wanted revenge on Larryboy for all the times he had foiled her plans to take more. With her and Awful Alvin's combined villainous minds, they would finally be able to defeat Larryboy once and for all. This time she was sure of it!

She just wished that Awful Alvin didn't feel the need to do that silly dance all the time.

CHAPTER 4

LITTLE RED SCHNUGGLY-PUGGLY

The staff of *The Daily Bumble* was working late that night. It was hard at work providing Bumblyburg with up-to-date news every morning in time for their breakfast pastries and toast. Especially when there was a big, gigantic, spectacular story like there was today.

Bob the Tomato's mother was coming to Bumblyburg for a visit! This was big news!

Well, at least Bob thought it was. And since Bob was the editor of *The Daily Bumble,* his mom was front page news.

Bob hopped over to the desk where photographer, Vicki Cucumber, and cub reporter, Junior Asparagus, were working. "Here's a picture of my mom playing Parcheesi with a pigeon," he said. "Or, here's a picture of her juggling violins at the State Fair. Which do you think we should print on the front page?"

Vicki and Junior looked at each other. Bob loved his mother. All tomatoes do. But they thought it was a bit silly that the editor of a newspaper still allowed his mom to call him,

"My little red schnuggly-puggly!"

But before Vicki and Junior had a chance to respond, Bob saw something out the window.

"Hey!" he said. "Are those flying pigs?"

The flying pigs circled around. They had locked in *The Daily Bumble* building as the next target of their pork–products assault. They hovered midair as the compartments on their wings opened and large sausages emerged, ready to be fired.

Bob, Vicki, and Junior watched the pigs through the window, unaware of the danger they were in. Vicki began snapping pictures. Maybe, just maybe, she could convince Bob that a picture of flying pigs was more newsworthy than a picture of his juggling mother.

"Something's coming out of their wings," said Junior. "I think it's...it's...Polish sausages!"

Larryboy had also seen the meaty weapons emerge from the wings of the pigs. "Archie!" he said. "They're gonna shoot Polish Sausage Torpedoes at *The Daily Bumble*!"

"Oh dear me!" said Archie. "You have to find some way to stop them!"

"OINK! OINK!" went the pigs.

Then each of the pigs fired two sausage torpedoes, sending six meats of destruction right at Bob, Vicki, and Junior.

"Yikes!" howled Larryboy.

It was too late for clever planning or anything like that. So, Larryboy did the only thing he could do: he dove the Larryplane right into the path of the sausage.

HE IS THAT HERO!

The Larryplane took six direct hits of spicy meat. This was just too much for even the advanced circuitry of the Larryplane's Automatic Anti-Closed-Eyes-Crash System. The Larryplane spun out of control. It was all Larryboy could do to steer away from the large buildings. He decided to try and make a crash landing in the Bumblyburg City Park, since there probably wouldn't be anyone there at this time of night.

CHAPTER 5

A CRASH COURSE IN CRASHING

But, as the Larryplane lurched through
the maze of buildings in downtown Bumblyburg, a solitary dark figure appeared atop a
nearby building. This figure was not laughing (nor
was he lamp-shaped, in case you were wonder-
ing.) The dark figure spread his cape and soared to
the ground of the city park.

"Larryboy! Eject! Eject!" Archie shouted.

"I can't find the button!" said Larryboy. Archie had
never thought to install an "Automatic-Eject-Larryboy-
If-His-Eyes-Are-Closed-Again-System" to eject
Larryboy by remote control.

"It's the blue button with the yellow star."

"I can't see it anywhere!" said Larryboy.

Larryboy's eyes were closed again.

"Open your eyes!" Archie told him.

Larryboy bravely peeked out from under his
eyelids and whispered, **"I AM THAT HERO!"** as
he fired both of his plunger ears, hitting a
tree to each side of him. The ropes went
taut and the plane plummeted to a
bouncing halt, inches off

the ground.

"WOW!" shouted Larryboy. "That was close!"

Larryboy released the ropes from his headpiece, and he and the plane dropped the last several inches to the ground.

"Larryboy, look out! The pigs are coming in for another attack!" shrieked Archie.

At that very moment, the dark figure shot out one of his talons from his belt and used it to swing across the sky. "Iyem...de Dark Crow!"

Who was this talon-bearing creature with a Spanish accent?

CHAPTER 6

SOMETHING TO CROW ABOUT

His name? Dark Crow.

He is a red grape that wears a black superhero costume that looks like a crow. He is the protector of the small, farming community of Maisefield. He is also a grape. But for some reason, Dark Crow doesn't like being a grape...that's why he took on the name Dark Crow. His crow-like supersuit and crow-like supergadgets give him a variety of ways to fight evildoers. Dark Crow takes crime-fighting *very* seriously. Larryboy knows him from the Superheroes Class at Bumblyburg Community College.

Dark Crow didn't think that Larryboy took super-heroing seriously enough. Not nearly seriously enough. But Larryboy was a superhero, none-the-less. And so, Dark Crow felt compelled to help one of his brothers in need.

"CA-CAW!"

"OINK! OINK!" the pigs called as Dark Crow swooped down in front of them.

The pigs veered to the side and circled around for another attack.

"Hello, Laddybuoy," said Dark Crow turning to face him. "Go home now. Get some rest, because theese case ees not big enough for the two of us."

"Huh?" said Larryboy who was oiling his ejector button with canola oil. "There! Good as new...ooops!"

The ejector seat fired and lunged Larryboy into the air. Fortunately for Dark Crow, Larryboy's ejector seat shot right into one of the flying pig's wings and smashed it all to bits.

With one wing ruined, the pig spun off and ricocheted into the other two flying pigs, ruining their wings as well. And without their hi-tech flying wings, the pigs weren't able to fly. They all fell with a **SPLASH** into Bumblyburg Park Lake.

Dark Crow rushed to the edge of the lake, pulled three small packets from his utility belt, and threw them to the pigs. The packets quickly inflated into black life-preservers with beaks and wings...just like a crow. The pigs grasped the life-preservers and floated to shore.

"Hey there, Dark Crow, good thing I ejected into those pigs. Otherwise, you might'a had a cowl full of bacon, huh?" asked Larryboy as he floated to the ground, thanks to the ejector seat's parachute. Unfortunately, the parachute got caught in a tree, and Larryboy was left dangling several feet from the ground.

"Are you kidding me? They never would haff snuck up on me eef I hadn't been busy saving you. They wouldn't stand a chance against...de Dark Crow!" Dark Crow said with a very Spanish accent and without a trace of friendliness in his voice.

Larryboy unhooked himself from his ejector seat and fell to the ground with an "Oof!" Then, he hopped after Dark Crow. "Well, thanks for saving me from the last pig attack. That was really...super."

"Look, Larryboy," Dark Crow scowled at him. "I saved you because eet's part of the superhero code. But why don't you just leave me alone now. You're messing up my case!"

"*Your* case?" asked Larryboy.

"That's right," said Dark Crow. "Awful Alvin and Greta Von Gruesome kidnapped those pigs from Maiseville yesterday, and I tracked them here to Bumblyburg."

"Greta Von Gruesome and Awful Alvin!" exclaimed Larryboy. "Lampy too?"

"Yes, Lampy too."

"Well, since they came to Bumblyburg, I can help you catch them!" said Larryboy with an excited smile on his face.

Dark Crow turned around angrily. He had no intentions of sharing his case with Larryboy, or anyone else for that matter. "I don't need any help! Just stay out of my way!"

"But...," said Larryboy as he was interrupted by the sound of Archie's voice coming over the communicator in his ear.

"Larryboy," said Archie, "an alarm has just gone off at the Bumblyburg Science Labs. Looks like a break-in. You better check it out."

"A break-in at the Bumblyburg Science Labs!" asked Larryboy.

Dark Crow spun back around as he heard this. "Egads! It must be Awful Alvin and Greta. Those flying peeegs were simply a big fat distraction to keep us *muy occupado* while they committed their villainous crimes! I haff to stop them!"

"Great!" Larryboy told him. "We can stop them together."

"Together? I giggle about this loudly in your peeekle juices!"

"I'm a cucumber!"

"De Dark Crow needs help from no-vegetable!" he said and was gone. He had disappeared into the night.

"Hey, wait up!" called Larryboy. "Could I catch a ride? My Larryplane's gonna be in the shop awhile!"

CHAPTER 7

THIS LITTLE LAMPY OF MINE

Dark Crow was right. Greta, Awful Alvin, and Lampy had broken into the Bumblyburg Science Labs after using the flying pigs as a distraction. And now, their villainous plan was in full swing! The scientists were all tied up, and Greta and Awful Alvin were pushing a giant telescope across the floor.

"How is this going to help us crack open the Mega–Safe?" asked Greta.

"Leave that to my dependable sidekick!" Awful Alvin snickered.

"Lampy? What can *he* do?" asked Greta as they placed the telescope in front of the Mega–Safe, which held the Bumblyburg Science Labs' most experimental and dangerous science projects.

Awful Alvin pointed the small end of the telescope at the safe, then put Lampy in front of the big end. "Lampy isn't just here for his pretty face and winning attitude," he told her. "He also has his own superpowers! I call it his 'Lampy Laser'!"

Alvin grabbed

Lampy's cord and prepared to plug it in. "This little lamp of mine," he sang, "I'm gonna let him shine!"

He plugged Lampy in, and Lampy's light flicked on, throwing light into the telescope. The telescope focused Lampy's light into a powerful beam, and began burning a hole in the Mega-Safe. "I'm gonna let him shine, let him shine, let him shine, let him shine!" Greta winced. Not another song and dance from Alvin!

Awful Alvin began dancing as he sang with glee. "Hide him under a bushel? NO! I'm gonna let him shine!"

Greta Von Gruesome sighed. Working with Awful Alvin was going to be about as much fun as working with a truck full of angry bees.

"Burn a hole in the Mega-Safe! I'm gonna let him shine! Burn a hole in the..."

There was a sound from above, and Awful Alvin stopped his singing. He and Greta looked up to see Dark Crow crash through the skylight in the ceiling.

"Dark Crow!" said Greta.

"That's right, dastardly doers!" crowed Dark Crow as his cape spread out like a bird, and he floated to the ground. "This crow's about to put a scare in you!"

Dark Crow whipped out his Crow-Yo (a yo-yo shaped like a crow). It zipped across the room and wrapped around Lampy's cord. Dark Crow yanked, and pulled the cord from the wall, thus shutting down the Lampy Laser.

Greta Von Gruesome fired a bolt of energy from her power gloves. But Dark Crow was too fast for her. He dodged the blast and leapt up onto the telescope, and twirled two Crow-Yo's over his head with his supersuit talons.

Then, with refined skill, Dark Crow flicked the double Crow-Yo's across the room at Greta and Awful Alvin, wrapping them up, back to back.

"Don't just stand there, Lampy," said Awful Alvin. "Get him!"

But Lampy didn't move. Alvin assumed he was waiting for the right moment.

Dark Crow ignored Lampy and leapt down from the telescope, and stood in front of the safe. "What are you criminals doing here?" he demanded. "What's in that safe that you wanted so badly?"

"We'll never tell!" said Awful Alvin.

"Oh yeah?" said Dark Crow. "Maybe I should see if Lampy will talk."

"NO!" said Awful Alvin. "Leave Lampy alone! He's villainous and all, but he'll never stand up to pressure! I'll tell you what you want to know!"

"Now we're getting somewhere," Dark Crow smirked.

CHAPTER 8

LARRYBOY LENDS A HAND

But just then, Larryboy rode up on the Larry-Unicycle, huffing and puffing mightily. **"I...AM...(PUFF, PUFF) THAT...(PUFF) HER...(PUFF, PUFF)...O!**

"Laddybuoy!" said Dark Crow. "What are you doing here? I haff things all rapid up here!"

"Not entirely," Larryboy told him as he picked up Lampy's unplugged cord. "This loose cord is a safety hazard. A good superhero always takes time to prevent accidents!"

"Laddybuoy! No!" shouted Dark Crow. But it was too late. Larryboy plugged Lampy back in, thus turning the Lampy Laser back on!

The Lampy Laser hit Dark Crow square in the chest, sending him flying backwards into the safe. He bounced off and crashed into Larryboy, sending them both sailing across the room, where they landed in a large vat of Sticky Scientific Goo (used for sticky scientific stuff).

Now that Dark Crow wasn't holding onto the Crow-Yo strings, Greta and Alvin were able to free themselves easily. "Thanks, Larryboy," said Greta. "We couldn't have escaped and continued our wicked plan without you!"

"You're welcome!" said Larryboy. "Oh...wait. You're *not* welcome!"

As Larryboy and Dark Crow sloshed around in the goo, Awful Alvin finished cutting a hole in the Mega Safe with the Lampy Laser.

When the hole was done, Awful Alvin and Greta rushed into the safe and wheeled out what looked like a laser canon. But it wasn't, it was the latest experimental wheel-mounted ray-gun invention of the Bumblyburg Science Labs!

"Now that we have this, no one will be able to stop us!" Greta said with glee. "Not even you pathetic 'super-heroes'!"

"And since no one can stop us, we will be unstoppable!" laughed Awful Alvin. "And since we are unstoppable, you can't stop us! Ha ha ha ha!"

Suddenly, he stopped laughing and got a weird look in his eye. "Ooh! I can feel another villainy dance coming on!"

"Oh give it a rest!" Greta Von Gruesome told him as she grabbed him by the arm and pulled him out the door.

CHAPTER 9

PROFESSOR FLURBLEBLUB SHARES SOME INFORMATION

Several minutes later, Larryboy and Dark Crow finally managed to pull themselves out of the vat of Sticky Scientific Goo. They untied the scientists.

"Thanks for untying us," said one of the scientists. "I'm Professor Flurbleblub, head of research here at the Labs."

"I've got Sticky Scientific Goo in my underpants," said Larryboy.

Ignoring Larryboy, Dark Crow turned to the professor. "What was that thing they stole?"

"It was one of our top-secret experiments!" replied Professor Flurbleblub.

"Eef it was top secret, how deed those villains know about it?" asked Dark Crow.

"Well, we think one of them may have been spying on us!" said Professor Flurbleblub. "Here, look at this surveillance photo." He showed Larryboy and Dark Crow a picture of Lampy wearing dark sunglasses and a fake moustache. "The thing they stole was our highly experimental Over-Easy-Egg Ray. It emits a special beam that can turn any inanimate object into over-easy eggs!"

"What's an inanimate object?" asked Larryboy.

"An inanimate object is anything that isn't alive," explained Professor Flurbleblub. "Like a rock, or a wall, or a car."

"But will they..."

Larryboy interrupted Dark Crow. "What about a cow?"

"Cows are alive," said Professor Flurbleblub. "The ray wouldn't work on a cow."

"What about a dead cow?"

"OK, a dead cow. The ray would turn a dead cow into over-easy eggs," Professor Flurbleblub conceded.

"Dastardly!" exclaimed Larryboy.

"Why would you even invent such a ray?" asked Dark Crow.

"Well...we don't always have time to make breakfast before we come to work," Professor Flurbleblub replied, sheepishly. "We're also working on a radioactive chamber to turn old hats into bagels and cream cheese."

"I like cream *and* cheese!" said Larryboy.

"So you're saying that with that ray, Greta and Awful Alvin will be able to turn anything they want eento over-easy eggs?" asked Dark Crow.

"Not anything," Larryboy corrected. "They can't turn cows into over-easy eggs."

"Unfortunately, most anything, yes," said Professor Flurbleblub. "The potential for badness just boggles the mind."

"Ees there anything you can do to stop them?" asked Dark Crow.

"Well, we did invent a special metal called 'Egganium' that is unaffected by the Over-Easy-Egg Ray," said Professor Flurbleblub. "If we didn't invent 'Egganium', we would have probably have turned the entire lab into over-easy-eggs by now! If you can give us some time, I believe we could think of a way to use that to stop the villains."

"Theese is all your fault, Laddybuoy!" said Dark Crow. "Eef you hadn't burst een on my case, those evildoers wouldn't haff that eggamatic weapon een their hands right now!"

"*Your* case?" said Larryboy. "But you're forgetting, this is *my* city!"

"Why don't you just share the case?" suggested Professor Flurbleblub. "Wouldn't God want you to share?"

"Share a case with Laddybuoy?" Dark Crow asked. "You must be joking."

"That's not a joke," said Larryboy. "Here's a joke! What do you get when you cross a water balloon with a porcupine?"

"Theese is no time for joking, Laddybuoy! Just stay out of my way! Theese case ees *mine*. I don't want to see you again until theese case ees over!"

"What about tomorrow night? That's when we have our Superhero Class together. I'll probably see you then," smiled Larryboy.

Dark Crow didn't answer, he just growled and gritted his teeth.

CHAPTER 10

NOW BOK CHOY
SHARES SOME INFORMATION

The next night at Superhero Class, Larryboy and Dark Crow tried to sit as far apart as they could. But it wasn't far enough to protect them from the cold stares they received from each other.

"As we all know, sharing is very important!" said Bok Choy, the teacher of the Superhero Class. "This is something most of us learned in kindergarten."

Dark Crow glared at Larryboy. Larryboy glared back. Neither of them was really paying attention to Bok Choy.

"Why, I remember my kindergarten teacher, Miss Loochy," Bok Choy sighed wistfully. "Sometimes the bigger kids wouldn't let me use the microscopes. But Miss Loochy always said, 'OK, class! I want you to share!' I loved Miss Loochy. I thought that I would marry her when I grew up..."

Bok Choy continued as he stared off into space with a silly grin on his face.

Suddenly, a mechanical arm shot out from Dark

Crow and dangled a paper in front of Larryboy. Larryboy leaned forward and looked at the crude drawing of himself with odor lines wafting away from him. The note read, "Larryboy = Stinkiness."

Larryboy was stunned by the rude gesture! He turned and gave Dark Crow a sour look as his extension arm retracted back into his helmet.

The look on Bok Choy's face had turned sour, too. "But then, Miss Loochy went off and married the principal, *Mr. Moochy! Ooooh!* I never liked Mr. Moochy! She should have married me! After all, I became a famous superhero!!"

Larryboy fired a plunger ear that stopped short of Dark Crow who looked stunned to see the plunger hovering in front of his face. Then with a **THWOPPING** sound, a balled up paper wad shot out of the plunger and struck Dark Crow in the forehead. Dark Crow's eyes briefly crossed as he looked up at the paper wad and then leered angrily at Larryboy.

"Master Choy!" said Dark Crow. "I haff a question! What should you do eef your *brilliant* plan to apprehend multiple super-villains ees bungled by an uninvited, second-rate cucumber een purple spandex?"

"You are *not* listening to the heart of my lesson!" said Bok Choy. "To have a sharing heart doesn't just mean sharing toys or jellybeans, or even microscopes. There are many times when sharing is important. Sharing blame, sharing work, sharing responsibilities. In all these things you must also share!"

"Oh, but I have a question too," said Larryboy. "What if the town that is under your sworn protection is invaded by a super-sulker, seedless grape who thinks he's a bird!"

"Who are you calling seedless?" Dark Crow warned.

"Larryboy! Dark Crow!" said Bok Choy. "You *both* need to hear the words of my lesson and take them to heart! Heroes! Turn in your Superhero Handbooks to Section Twenty-One, Paragraph Four, Subsection Nine and Ten. 'Two are better than one because they have a good return for their work; If one falls down, his friend can help him up!'"

As Bok Choy was speaking, Dark Crow fired a talon-line from his utility belt. It whipped around an overhead light and dropped down behind Larryboy, attaching to his pants. The talon tugged and gave Larryboy a superwedgie, lifting him momentarily out of his seat. When the cable released, Larryboy fell back to his seat with a loud *thud*.

"OOOOP!"

"When two work together, they are stronger than one," Bok Choy said sternly, looking from Larryboy to Dark Crow. "Learn today's lesson! And your many questions shall be answered."

CHAPTER 11

LARRY SCOFFS AT THE SCOOP

The next day, Larryboy's
alter ego, Larry the Janitor, reported
for work at *The Daily Bumble*. The
reporters at *The Daily Bumble* always
seemed to know everything that was going on
in Bumblyburg, so posing as a janitor was a good
way for Larryboy to pick up important information.

As Larry mopped the floor, Vicki Cucumber
strolled by. Larry thought that Vicki was the most
beautiful cucumber in all of Bumblyburg. If he could
just muster the courage to invite her to the Founder's
Day Party!

"Good morning, Vicki," he said. "What's the scoop
today?"

"Well, it looks like Larryboy tried to break up a
break-in at the Bumblyburg Science Labs last night,"
she explained as she showed him a copy of the
morning paper.

Larry looked at the front page. Larryboy's picture was on the front. But guess whose picture
was there right alongside his...Dark Crow!

"Looks like he had some help from Dark Crow, the dark grape from Maisefield," said Vicki. Larry frowned. The picture of Dark Crow was bigger than the picture of Larryboy!

"Why should I...um...I mean why should *Larryboy*

have to share the front page with Dark Crow? Larryboy is Bumblyburg's favorite and most handsome sworn defender! That Dark Crow is just a hero-come-lately! Why, he couldn't even carry Larryboy's..."

Just then Larry's mop rang. "What's that?" asked Vicki.

"Um, nothing."

"No, I heard something," said Vicki.

"Yeah, now I hear it too," Larry agreed. "I think it's the sound of a toilet about to overflow. I better go take care of it, since I am the janitor and all."

"Ok. I'm on my way to the museum for a photo shoot, anyway. See you later, Larryboy!" Vicki called after him. But Larryboy was already gone.

Larry hopped into the janitor closet. He knew that the beeping was coming from his mop. Archie had installed a communicator in Larry's mop to contact him when there was a Larryboy emergency. But Larryboy really needed to talk to Archie about the beeping. Sometimes, it could be *really* embarrassing.

Larry threw the mop over his head, thus activating the video screen that linked him to Archie in the Larrycave. "Master Larry, I have some terrible news," said Archie. "Awful Alvin, Greta Von Gruesome, and Lampy have just been spotted outside of the Bumblyburg Museum of History and Old Stuff."

"I bet they're there to check out the mummy exhibit," said Larryboy. "I've been meaning to go see it myself!"

"Not likely. I suspect that they have nothing but mischief on their warped minds! This looks like a job for Larryboy!"

CHAPTER 12

TWO PHARAOHS AND A QUEEN

The Bumblyburg Museum of History and Old Stuff contained several priceless old things made of gold and jewels. As a result, every super-villain worth their wicked cackle wanted to break in and steal the Old Stuff.

But the walls of the museum were protected with reinforced steel and concrete. No super-villain had ever broken in.

That was about to change.

Awful Alvin hovered outside the museum walls on his hovering platform. It was one of the things that his awful mind had invented. It was handy to float around town and to hover above someone's head if he wanted to dump a bucket of soapy water on them. But now, he was using it for something different. He had hooked the Over-Easy-Egg Ray to the platform, and was hovering just outside the Museum of History and Old Stuff with Greta and Lampy onboard as well.

"**HA HA HA,**" laughed Awful Alvin. "Mere

walls can't keep us out now that we have the power of the Over-Easy-Egg Ray!

"**FIRE!**" commanded Greta.

"Would it kill you to say, 'please'?" asked Awful Alvin.

Inside the museum, Mrs. Celery was leading her class through the mummy exhibit just as Vicki arrived to take pictures.

Junior posed beside a mummy-wrapped asparagus and said, "Take this shot! My headline can be, 'Me and My Mummy!'"

Bob just grumbled. "That's fine for a school newspaper, Junior. But it's not the kind of story that sells in Bumblyburg. I wish something exciting would happen around here."

"And here we have the royal clothing of Pharaoh Edward Potatothep of Ancient Egypt," Mrs. Celery said as she led the group over to a small sphinx, that was just about her height. "And this was the Pharaoh's sphinx."

"Did you say the Pharaoh stinks?" asked Junior Asparagus.

"No, no! The Pharaoh's sphinx!"

But before Mrs. Celery had a chance to fully explain, the room was filled with a **WOBBLE-WOBBLE** sort of sound.

"What is that noise?" asked Mrs. Celery.

A moment later, her question was answered, as the wall of the museum turned to over-easy eggs right before their very eyes, and fell down on top of her and her students.

"Yuck! Over-easy eggs!" said one of the students.

Another student shrugged and took a bite. "Better than cafeteria lunch."

Awful Alvin, Greta, and Lampy floated into the room on the floating platform.

"It's Awful Alvin and Greta Von Gruesome!" shouted Mrs. Celery as she wiped the eggs from her eyes. "Run children! Run!"

The children just stood and stared at her. "Um, I mean, line up and file out in an orderly fashion, please," she clarified. "But do it quickly!" And the children did just that. They were very good little students.

"HA HA HA HA HA!" laughed Awful Alvin, who was neither good nor little. "Finally, the forbidden treasures of the Bumblyburg Museum shall be mine! All mine! All miney-meanie-miney-mo-mine!"

"What do you mean 'all yours'?" said Greta. "I get my share, too!"

"Of course, of course," said Awful Alvin as he grabbed the royal headdress of Pharaoh Potatophep and placed it on his own head. "Look at me! I'm a Pharaoh! Pharaoh Alvin!" he gloated as he placed another headdress on Lampy. "Look at us! Two Pharaohs out on the town! Lookin' sharp! Check us out, the coolest Pharaohs you ever will meet! Oh yeah!" Awful Alvin grabbed Lampy and strutted around the museum floor.

Using some velvet rope from one of the exhibits, Greta and Alvin tied up Bob, Vicki, and Junior.

"You'll never get away with this! Larryboy will stop you!" Vicki said as she glared at the menacing duo.

"Hey, Lampy!" said Alvin. "I've got an idea! Let's give ourselves a big Pharaoh cheer!" He set Lampy down and began waving his arms wildly like a cheerleader. **"GIMME AN 'F'... 'F!' GIMME AN 'A'... 'A!' GIMME AN 'R'... 'R!' GIMME AN 'O'... 'O!' GIMME A 'W'... 'W!' WHAT DOES IT SPELL?"** he called out.

But no one said anything.

"Lampy, what does is spell?"

Lampy didn't say anything.

"It spells FAROW!" said Awful Alvin. "Gooo Farows!"

"That's not how you spell Pharaoh!" said Vicki.

"You're just jealous that you don't get to be in our Farow Club!" said Alvin as he looked to Lampy for agreement. "Oh, Lampy, doesn't this villainy just make you feel like..."

Greta whirled around, cutting Alvin off, "One more dance step and I'll serve you on toast with a side of bacon!"

"Now this is what I call news!" said Bob, as he tried to

wiggle free from the ropes that kept him bound.

"If I could get free, I could snap a front page photo of the villains!" Vicki added.

Greta hopped over to the other side of the museum and used her power gloves to blast through the protective glass surrounding Queen Loopy Goop the Fourth's royal crown. She placed the crown on her head. "All shall bow! Bow before your queen!" she said, addressing her imaginary subjects. She put on the queen's robes, grabbed the queen's royal scepter, and sat in the queen's royal throne. "Now bring the queen some honey-roasted peanuts! And somebody scratch my back in that spot I can never reach! Your queen commands it!"

Before long, all three of them were dressed from top to bottom in the most expensive royal clothing in all history. They started loading all kinds of gold and jewels on Alvin's floating platform to take with them when they left. Of course, both Alvin and Greta were planning to trick each other and keep all the riches for themselves, but for now, they were just having too much fun stealing stuff to think about that!

Greta approached a mummy's tomb, giddy with excitement. "I wonder what's in here!" she cackled. "Probably filled with diamonds and rubies…or maybe a fondue set. I love fondue!"

Greta used the queen's scepter to pry the tomb open. But when she opened it, she saw no jewels. Instead, all she heard was…

"CA-CAW!"

CHAPTER 13

OVER-EASY-EGG RAY UNLEASHED!

"Prepare to eat crow-bar!" said Dark Crow as he whipped out his crow-bar, preparing to ensnare the villains once again. "I knew you two couldn't resist trying to rob the museum!"

But Greta was too quick for him this time and knocked the crowbar away with the scepter. "Prepare to bow before your queen, peasant!" said Greta as she swung the scepter at Dark Crow.

Just then, the Larrymobile drove in through the over-easy-egg hole in the wall. **"I AM THAT HERO!"** Larryboy exclaimed as he leapt from his supercar.

"Laddybuoy!" said Dark Crow. "I thought I told you to stay out of theese!"

"You can't just claim a case in my city and… look out!"

Larryboy's warning came just in time. Dark Crow blocked another blow from Greta's scepter with the crowbar. But he was off balance, and tripped, causing him to roll across the room and crash into a large pillar. The pillar began to tip and fell right toward Bob, Vicki, and Junior!

"Larryboy! Help!" cried Vicki.

Larryboy whirled around and shot a plunger ear which attached to Bob's forehead. The rope went taut and Larryboy pulled the tied-up trio out from under the pillar just seconds before the pillar crashed to floor.

"Let's get out of here!" Bob said to Junior as they quickly hopped out the hole in the over-easy wall.

Vicki spun out of the velvet ropes and twirled right into Larryboy's......arms?

"Vicki, I want to ask you something about the Founder's Day Party," Larryboy said as the words tumbled out before he even knew he'd said them.

"Oh Larryboy! What is it?" she asked, looking dreamily into his eyes.

"Um...this year...are they going to have refreshments like hot fudge sundaes at the party?" he said with a somewhat squeaky voice.

"Did you say, party? I was born to party!" Dark Crow chimed in as Spanish music surrounded him.

Larryboy turned to face Dark Crow. "Hey! Ya mind?"

"Yes, I *do* mind, Laddybuoy! I had things under control here before you arrived!" said Dark Crow.

"Did not!" said Larryboy.

"Did too!"

"Did not with lemons on top!"

"Sorry to interrupt your strategic superhero planning session," said a voice from above them. They both looked up to see Awful Alvin and Lampy looking down at them from the floating platform. The Over-Easy-Egg Ray was pointed right at them. "I just thought you might like to be made aware that you're about to be the victims of a concentrated blast of pure villainy!"

"We know all about your Over-Easy-Egg Ray!" said Dark Crow. "It can't hurt us!"

"Yeah," agreed Larryboy. "We're not a laminated object!"

"In*animate* object!" corrected Dark Crow.

"That's what I said," said Larryboy.

"No, it wasn't."

"Besides, we're not wooden cows!" Larryboy said, finishing the argument.

"You're right," interrupted Alvin, who was getting tired of the heroes always talking when he wanted to taunt and mock them. "It won't work on you. But I think it will

work quite well on your supersuits!"

Larryboy and Dark Crow's eyes went wide. Their super crime-fighting costumes!

OH NO!

WOBBLE-WOBBLE! Awful Alvin zapped them. Larryboy and Dark Crow looked at one another.

"Better quiche your super-costumes goodbye!" Greta cackled.

"Um....you're covered in eggs," said Larryboy.

"So are you," Dark Crow pointed out.

Awful Alvin and Greta laughed.

"You won't get away with this!" said Larryboy. He turned his head to fire his plunger ear, but the result was a lump of eggs that fell off the side of his head. Even his plungers had been turned to eggs!

"Sorry, Larryboy!" said Greta. "We *will* get away with it! We will get away with all the loot we can carry! We're even taking the Pharaoh's sphinx!"

"Did you say the Pharaoh stinks?" asked Larryboy.

"No! The Pharaoh's sphinx!"

"I really don't think that's what you said," Larryboy told her.

"That sphinx is property of honest and good citizens!" said Dark Crow. "I'll stop you, costume or no costume!" He leapt toward Green Greta, but she blasted him with her power gloves, sending him rolling back into the mummy's tomb. Then Greta hopped back up onto the floating platform, and prepared to exit.

"See you later, super zeroes," said Awful Alvin. "Maybe you better run home to your mummy! Ha ha ha! Get it? Mummy?"

The villains swooped past Vicki who had just bent over to pick up her camera. Seeing Vicki gave Alvin another awful idea. He reached over and scooped her onto the platform.

"You two super-losers had better let us go about our villainous villainy or the newspaper gal gets egged!"

"LARRYBOY! HEEEEELLLLPPP!" Vicki screamed as the villains flew out the museum with Vicki on board.

CHAPTER 14

A COSTUME PARTY

Once the villains left, Larryboy and Dark Crow realized they couldn't just go around trying to catch super-villains wearing nothing but over-easy eggs. They had to wipe the egg off their faces and get back to work!

Fortunately, Larryboy found a bag of clothes in a dumpster in the alley behind the Museum. *Unfor*tunately, the bag of clothes contained nothing but fuzzy pajamas.

Larryboy chose fuzzy yellow pj's with teddy bears, while Dark Crow chose fuzzy green pj's with race cars. It was the best they could do.

Then Larryboy had an idea that they should also wear paper bags over their heads to protect their secret identities. Dark Crow thought this was a good idea, but he did suggest that they cut eyeholes in the bags so they could see. Larryboy reluctantly agreed.

Once they had changed into their new "costumes",

Larryboy hopped out from behind a dumpster. "How do I look?" he asked.

"You look ridiculous," said Dark Crow.

"So do you," said Larryboy.

They were both right.

But Larryboy brightened when he found an old plunger in the dumpster. He carefully tied it to his head. "This will help everyone know that it's me...Larryboy."

"I don't know about theese new costumes," said Dark Crow. "They don't exactly strike fear into the hearts of evildoers everywhere. Maybe we should go home and get

our spare costumes."

"You can go home if you want," said Larryboy. "But Greta and Awful Alvin have Vicki! I have no time to be concerned about fashion!"

Dark Crow agreed. (He wasn't about to let Larryboy capture the villains by himself and take all the credit.) They decided they should return to the Bumblyburg Science Labs. Maybe Professor Flurbleblub and the other scientists had come up with a way to defeat the Over-Easy-Egg Ray.

CHAPTER 15

THE BUNNY-BOT 3000

Larryboy and Dark Crow
made their way over to the Science
Labs. Once Professor Flurbleblub and the
other scientists stopped laughing at their
new costumes, they took the heroes down to
the high-security sub-basement of the labs and
stood them in front of a large metal door.

"Have you figured out a way to stop the
Over-Easy-Egg Ray?" asked Larryboy.

"We hope so," said Professor Flurbleblub. "We took
the Egganium and used it to create…this!"

He pressed a button, and the large metal door slid
open to reveal…a giant metal bunny.

"You created a mega-bunny?" asked Dark Crow.

"It's the ultimate Over-Easy-Egg Fighting robot
suit!" said Professor Flurbleblub. "The Bunny-Bot
3000! You get inside and control the robot's move-
ments."

"But, why would you shape it like a bunny?"
asked Larryboy.

"Well…we think bunnies are real cute,"

Professor Flurbleblub answered sheepishly. "There's just one problem. We only had enough Eggananium to make one Bunny-Bot. You'll have to share."

"Share?" asked a stunned Dark Crow. "No-hip-hop-ping-bunny-trailing-way! Theese is *my* case!"

"But it's *my* city!" said Larryboy.

"You know, you are right, Laddybuoy. By the way, your shoe's untied!" chuckled Dark Crow.

Larryboy looked down. "What? I'm not wearing any shoes. I don't even have any feet!"

"I know," said Dark Crow. But while Larryboy was looking for his shoes, Dark Crow had slipped into the Bunny-Bot. "Adios, Jammie-boy. Vicki, have no fear, de Dark Crow is coming to safe you!"

"Hey! No fair!" said Larryboy.

The rocket thrusters in the Bunny-Bot's feet fired up, and Dark Crow lifted off.

"You're not leaving without me!" called Larryboy. He jumped toward the robot with a big **KER-PLOK!** As he attached himself with the plunger that was tied to his head, the ceiling opened up and the Bunny-Bot's rocket thrusters roared to life. The scientists watched as they blasted through the roof.

"WHOOOOOOAAAAH!" said Larryboy.

CHAPTER 16

SHIMMYING WITH BADNESS

At that moment in downtown Bumblyburg, just beneath *The Daily Bumble* building, Mayor Flapjack's car was being turned into a big lump of gooey eggs. Moments later, a traffic light was turned into eggs. A telephone pole, a fountain, and a kissing booth, all turned to over-easy eggs.

Awful Alvin, Greta Von Gruesome, and Lampy were floating around town, randomly turning things into eggs. Just because they could. And just because they were bad.

"Sometimes, I simply love being bad!" said Awful Alvin. "And this is one of those times! My badness is like a tickle in my tummy that makes me want to shake and shimmy. Shimmy with badness! Shimmy with me Lampy!"

But just as Awful Alvin began to shimmy, there was a roar overhead. The villains looked up and saw something flying through the sky.

"Look, up in the sky!" said Greta.

"It's a weather balloon."

"It's a metallic flying fish!" thought Awful Alvin.

The Bunny-Bot 3000 zoomed toward the dastardly duo, with Larryboy still attached.

"WHHHOOOOORAAAAA!" said Larryboy.

"It's a cucumber wearing pajamas attached to a bunny-shaped robot," said Greta.

"It's Larryboy!" exclaimed Vicki.

The Bunny-Bot landed in front of the super-villains who were hovering a few feet off the ground. "Halt, you villains!" said Dark Crow from inside the bunny suit. "Your days of foul deeds are over!"

"Don't you mean over-*easy*?" said Greta.

She fired the Over-Easy-Egg Ray at the Bunny-Bot, fully expecting it to turn to eggs. But the Egganium stood firm and did not turn to egg. It remained distinctly un-egg-like!

"What!?" said Awful Alvin. "How can this be?"

"Looks like you're headed to prison to do some hard-*boiled* time!" boasted Dark Crow.

The Bunny-Bot's arms extended to the villains, and reached out to grab them with its metal claws.

Just then Larryboy hopped out from behind the robot in his pj's and paper bag. "Dark Crow! It's my turn to use the Bunny-Bot!" he cried.

"No way!" said Dark Crow.

"You got to fly it here!"

"That doesn't count!"

While the two heroes were arguing, Awful Alvin created another awful plan. He might not be able to turn the Bunny-Bot into eggs, but there was more than one way to defeat a super-hero.

Awful Alvin pointed the Over-Easy-Egg Ray up at the roof of *The Daily Bumble* building, and fired. **WOBBLE-WOBBLE!** The statue of a giant bumble bee atop the building turned to eggs and slid from the roof, falling to the street below.

"Of course it counts!" said Larryboy. "So now it's my tur..."

SPLAT!

Larryboy, Dark Crow, and the Bunny-Bot were trapped beneath two tons of over-easy eggs.

CHAPTER 17

A SKILLET SITUATION

When Larryboy and Dark Crow awoke, they were in Awful Alvin's lair. This is a bad place to be at any time. For one thing, this is where Awful Alvin usually is. For another thing, it smells really bad. But as if being in Awful Alvin's lair wasn't bad enough, Larryboy, Dark Crow, and Vicki all found themselves tied to the Pharaoh's sphinx. And if *that* wasn't bad enough, the sphinx was suspended from the ceiling. But wait, it gets worse! The sphinx was suspended above a giant skillet that was being heated by the Lampy Laser, while the Bunny-Bot stood uselessly in the corner. And to top it all off, Greta Von Gruesome and Awful Alvin (who were still wearing their stolen finery from the museum) had the Over-Easy-Egg Ray pointed right at them!

"Good morning, eggy heads!" said Greta.

"What's the meaning of theese?" demanded Dark Crow.

"Don't worry, Vicki. I'll get us out of this," Larryboy whispered.

"You? Ha!" Dark Crow...well, he crowed. "I

once again laugh een your vesh-a-table face. Only a fruit like me can safe us now!"

"Oh, that's quite unlikely!" said Awful Alvin. "You see, my plan is almost villainously simple!"

"With just a flick of the switch, the Over-Easy-Egg Ray turns that sphinx into a big glob of eggs," explained Greta. "Those eggs will plop down into the skillet. And since you're tied to the sphinx, you're about to become the world's biggest superhero and Vicki omelet!"

"I wanted to make a superhero quiche," said Awful Alvin. "But Greta said we didn't have a flaky enough crust for you two flakes!"

"Hokay, see how you mess up my plans! Make me wear paper bags over my head. My anger for you eese enraging largely, as we speak, my friend," Dark Crow said as he glowered at Larryboy.

"What about the way you try to take over my super-hero territory? AND the girl I'm inviting to the Founder's Day Party!"

Vicki's eyes widened and she smiled. But before she could speak, Dark Crow interrupted.

"Vicki, tell him that...de Dark Crow ees your favorite!" he said with a hop as Spanish music began to play...from somewhere.

"Both of you stop it! Look!" Vicki cried.

Greta and Alvin had approached the Egg Ray.

"Quiet, you two!" demanded Greta. "I think it's time for things to get cookin'!"

They were ready to seal the doom of the troubled trio forever.

CHAPTER 18

LARRYBOY AND DARK CROW
REALIZE SOMETHING

"And now, I will flip the switch and say goodbye forever!" said Greta.

"You?" challenged Awful Alvin. "I, Awful Alvin, the most villainous mind of our time should be allowed to finish them off!"

"Nay!" said Greta. "I've waited too long for this moment to let a smelly little onion flip the switch!"

"Such an awful deed as this should only be done by the most awful villain! And I, Awful Alvin, could out-awful you with one root behind my back!"

"Don't make me zap you with my power gloves!" warned Greta.

By this time, Larryboy and Dark Crow had stopped their own arguing to listen to the bickering bad guys.

"You know," Larryboy pointed out, "if they'd just quit arguing, they could have finished us off by now."

"How foolish they are!" said Dark Crow. "Eef they would simply share the task, they could haff feenished us off by now."

"Yeah! They'd both get what they wanted if they'd work together."

Suddenly, at the mere mention of the words "share and work together", both Larryboy and Dark Crow were reminded of the lesson that Bok Choy had been trying to teach them in superhero class. They remembered him saying, "When two work together, they are stronger than one."

"Laddybuoy," said Dark Crow. "I just realized something. We haff forgotten Master Choy's lesson. We should haff been sharing!"

"Yeah, sharing the responsibilities of catching the villains, and working together to capture them!" agreed Larryboy.

"Just like we should haff shared the blame when things went wrong."

"And the Bunny-bot suit."

"And our super-abilities," said Dark Crow. "Eef we had shared those things and worked together, we would haff caught the villains by now!"

"God likes it when we work together," Vicki added, trying to encourage her superheroes.

"Well, maybe it's not too late," said Larryboy. "If we share our abilities now, we might still have a chance of getting out of this mess! Let's work together!"

"Side by side, my friend!" agreed Dark Crow.

CHAPTER 19

SUCCESSFUL SHARING

"OK, OK!" said Awful Alvin. "Why don't we vote on who gets to flip the switch?"

"Lampy's vote doesn't count," said Greta.

"Of course it counts! He's heating the skillet!"

"Guys! I think if we can bump the telescope just right, we might have a chance. What do you think?" Vicki asked.

Larryboy and Dark Crow shot each other a look and then turned back to Vicki.

"You know, you're pretty sharp for someone who's never been to a superhero class!" Larryboy told her.

As the villains continued to argue about who would get to flip the switch, Larryboy and Dark Crow worked together to swing the sphinx back and forth.

They kept working together, swinging the sphinx farther and farther until...bump! They hit the telescope, causing it to spin around.

The focused light from Lampy shot across the room, hitting the Egganium coated Bunny-Bot which reflected the light across the room. The light then cut the rope that held the sphinx to the ceiling!

Since the sphinx was swinging back and forth, it flew away from the skillet, and landed on the hard floor. The sphinx shattered and the heroes were able to slip out of their bonds. They were free!

"Great shot, Laddybuoy!" said Dark Crow.

"You too!" said Larryboy. "We did it together!"

Unfortunately, the shattering of the sphinx on the floor was noisy enough to draw the attention of Greta and Awful Alvin. "They've escaped!" shrieked Greta.

"Get them!" yelled Alvin.

Larryboy and Dark Crow rushed to the Bunny-Bot as

the villains pushed each other out of the way in an attempt to get to the Over-Easy-Egg Ray.

"Who's turn is it?" asked Larryboy as they reached the Bunny-Bot.

"Eet's your turn, Laddybuoy," said Dark Crow. "After all I *deed* get to fly it here. So get inside while I draw their fire."

Dark Crow jumped out from behind the Bunny-Bot. "Hey! Over here! Nya-nya nya-nya blah-blah!"

"No one 'nya-nya's' Greta Von Gruesome!"

WOBBLE-WOBBLE! She fired the Over-Easy-Egg Ray at Dark Crow, but he was able to jump out of the way.

While Greta was busy with Dark Crow, Larryboy jumped inside the Bunny-Bot and it blinked to life.

Dark Crow continued hopping around, trying to distract Greta from what Larryboy was doing. "Nya-nya!" But he wasn't watching where he was going and ran into a wall. "Nya-nya, nya…oof!" He fell over and was trapped against the wall.

"Now I've got you!" said Greta. "Prepare for your precious pj's to become poultry progeny!"

"Poultry what?" asked Dark Crow.

"I said…oh never mind!" Greta fired the ray again. **WOBBLE-WOBBLE.**

But at the last instant, the Bunny-Bot, piloted by Larryboy, stepped in the way of the Over-Easy-Egg Ray and shielded Dark Crow. "Prepare to get 'beaten' villains!"

The hands of the Bunny-Bot transformed into eggbeaters which spun with a **WHIRRRRR!** Larryboy brought the eggbeater arms down on the Over-Easy-Egg Ray, scrambling it to pieces once and for all.

"That's my cucumber!" cheered Vicki.

"Drat," said Greta.

"Way to go, Laddybuoy!" said Dark Crow.

But Awful Alvin had managed to run for cover.

"We're not defeated yet!" sneered Awful Alvin! "Let's see if your robot is Lampy-Laser proof, too!"

Alvin fired the Lampy Laser at the Bunny-Bot, cutting through the robot's leg. (As it turns out, Egganium is very resistant to Over-Easy-Egg Rays, but otherwise, it's pretty worthless.) The Bunny-Bot fell to the floor.

"Yikes!" said Larryboy. "Where's the eject button? Shouldn't there be an eject button!"

"Get him, Lampy!" Alvin shouted. "You may have destroyed my Over-Easy-Egg Ray, but I can still destroy you!"

But before he could get off another shot, Dark Crow whipped his crow-yo out from his jammies and ensnared Lampy's cord. With one big yank, the cord was ripped from the wall. Then the crow-yo whipped back around the awful villains, trapping them tightly together.

Lampy spun, wiggled, and shook, causing all of them to topple over with a loud crash! Dark Crow swung one of his talon-lines and landed beside the bunny as Larryboy hopped out.

"Great working weeth you, pardner!" he said.

"Look! Greta is running for the door!" Vicki shrieked.

Larryboy turned to Dark Crow and together they were able to shoot Larryboy's makeshift plunger ear at the villian. Greta was encircled with a big **WHHOOOSH,** but she ducked just in time. Whirling toward the door, she taunted the superheroes as she hopped away. "Sorry, boys, you missed!"

Continuing to work together, the superheros once again shot Larryboy's improvised plunger and Dark Crow's crow-yo at the door and pulled. It forced Greta backward into a large vat of scientific goo.

"Sorry, evildoers," said Larryboy. "This time, things didn't turn out sunny-side up!"

CHAPTER 20

TRUTH AND SHARE

Later, with Greta Von Gruesome, Awful Alvin, and Lampy safely in jail, Larryboy and Dark Crow went back to the Bumblyburg Science Labs to return the telescope the villains had stolen. (But not before taking a moment to change into their spare costumes.)

Bob and Junior stood nearby as Vicki flashed pictures of the momentous event.

"Thank you," said Professor Flurbleblub. "This telescope is very important to us."

"Do you use it to look at faraway galaxies?" asked Larryboy?

"Sometimes," said Professor Flurbleblub. "Mostly we use it to help look for our lost car keys."

"Well, I have to share the credit with Dark Crow," Larryboy pointed out. "I couldn't have done it without him."

"And I couldn't have done eet without Laddybuoy. He taught me why sharing ees important...even for a superhero."

"Because when two people work together, they are more powerful than either one of them is alone!" Larryboy said, echoing the words of his superhero teacher.

"Oh, I can see the headline, now," Bob said. "'Teamwork Tosses Bad Guys' Salad!' Or maybe, 'United We Stand, Divided We Get Egg On Our Faces!' Or, or...."

As Bob decided which headline was best, Vicki made her way over to talk to her favorite superhero. "Was there something you wanted to ask me about Founder's Day, Larryboy?"

"Gosh. Founder's Day....Umm..." he said, pondering Vicki's words as he looked toward the sky. "Wow, drawing blanks here."

"Didn't you want to ask me to the Founder's Day Party, Larry?"

"**OOOOO....RRRRRRIIIIGHT,**" Larryboy stuttered.

"I'd love to go with you!"

"Wow! Really?" Larryboy said as they hopped out of the laboratory with Dark Crow close behind them.

"Maybe we could have a nice dinner together, first," Vicki suggested.

"Hey, Laddybuoy! We're a team, are we not?" Dark Crow called after them.

Vicki and Larryboy stopped and smiled as Dark Crow caught up to them.

"We must do *everything* together now. I will show you how to dance because I yem – de Dark Crow!" he said, striking a pose as Spanish music began to play.

"Where does that music come from?" Larryboy asked as they all hopped off together.

"I like you so much, Laddybuoy! No matter what anybody

else says about you. You know, I haff a very talented cho-
reographer you should meet. She does all my music," Dark
Crow told him. "Een fact, I am looking for a stunt double.
Think about it, Laddybuoy. I mean getting egged like we
did, ees not the way we should be seen by our public. No,
no no. We are superheroes, you and me….."

"Hey! Larryboy and Dark Crow didn't stay to see our
latest experiment," said Professor Flurbleblub. "And I think
they would have been so impressed. After all, no one else
has ever thought of inventing a set of wings that will help
pigs fly!"

Life was never easy for a superhero.

THE END

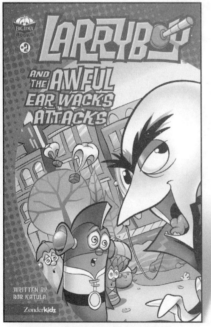